# THE MATS

*by Francisco Arcellana* ◆ *illustrated by Hermès Alègrè*

A CRANKY NELL BOOK

 Kane/Miller Book Publishers

Brooklyn, New York & La Jolla, California

First American Edition 1999 by Kane/Miller Book Publishers
Brooklyn, New York & La Jolla, California

"The Mats" first appeared as a short story in *Philippine Magazine* in 1938

Originally published in book form in the Philippines in 1995 by
Tahanan Books for Young Readers, Metro Manila, Philippines

Library of Congress Cataloging-in-Publication Data

Arcellana, Francisco.
The mats / by Francisco Arcellana ; illustrated by Hermès Alègrè.
—1st American ed.
p.  cm.
Summary: Marcelina's father comes home from a trip to Manila with beautiful
hand-made sleeping mats for each member of his large family,
including the three daughters who died when they were very young.
[1. Philippines—Fiction. 2. Family life—Philippines—Fiction.]
I. Alègrè, Hermès, 1968-  ill.  II. Title.
PZ7.A67435Mat  [E]—dc21  1999  98-35719

Printed and bound in Singapore by Tien Wah Press Pte. Ltd.
1 2 3 4 5 6 7 8 9 10

ISBN 0-916291-86-3

*Bless the little children.*
F. A.

*For my Sirena*
H. A.

For my family, Papa's homecoming from his many inspection trips around the Philippines was always an occasion to remember. But there was one homecoming—from a trip to the south—that turned out to be more memorable than any of the others.

Papa was an engineer. He inspected new telegraph lines for the government. He had written from Lopez, Tayabas:

*I have just met a marvelous matweaver—a real artist—and I shall have a surprise for you. I asked him to weave a sleeping mat for every one of the family. I can hardly wait to show them to you....*

After a few days Papa wrote again:

*I am taking the Bicol Express tomorrow. I have the mats with me, and they are beautiful. I hope to be home to join you for dinner.*

Mama read Papa's letter aloud during the noon meal. Talk about the mats flared up like wildfire.

"I like the feel of mats," said my brother Antonio. "I like the smell of new mats."

"Oh, but these mats are different," said Susanna, my younger sister. "They have our names woven into them. There is a different color for each of us."

A mat was not anything new to us. There was already one such mat in the house. It was one we seldom used, a mat older than any of us.

This mat had been given to Mama by her mother when Mama and Papa were married. It had been with them ever since. It was used on their wedding night and afterwards only on special occasions. It was a very beautiful mat. It had green leaf borders and gigantic red roses woven into it. In the middle it said:

*Emilia y Jaime*
*Recuerdo*

The mat did not ever seem to grow old. To Mama it was always as new as it had been on her wedding night. The folds and creases always looked new and fresh. The smell was always the smell of a new mat. Watching it was an endless joy.

Mama always kept that mat in her trunk. When any of us got sick, the mat was brought out and the sick child made to sleep on it. Every one of us had at some time in our life slept on it. There had been sickness in our family. And there had been deaths....

That evening Papa arrived. He had brought home a lot of fruit from the fruit-growing provinces he had passed in his travels. We sampled pineapple, lanzones, chico, atis, santol, watermelon, guayabano, and avocado. He had also brought home a jar of preserved sweets.

Dinner seemed to last forever. Although we tried not to show it, we could hardly wait to see the mats.

Finally, after a long time over his cigar, Papa rose from his chair and crossed the room. He went to the corner where his luggage was piled. From the heap he pulled out a large bundle. Taking it under his arm, he walked to the middle of the room where the light was brightest. He dropped the bundle to the floor. Bending over and balancing himself on his toes, he pulled at the cord that bound it. It was strong. It would not break. It would not give way. Finally, Alfonso, my youngest brother, appeared at Papa's side with a pair of scissors.

Papa took the scissors. One swift movement, *snip!*, and the bundle was loose!

Papa turned to Mama and smiled. "These are the mats, Miling," he said.

He picked up the topmost mat in the bundle.

"This is yours, Miling." Mama stepped forward to the light, wiping her still moist hands against the folds of her apron. Shyly, she unfolded the mat without a word.

We all gathered around the spread mat.

It was a beautiful mat. There was a name in the very center of it: Emilia. Interwoven into the large, green letters were flowers—*cadena de amor*.

"It's beautiful, Jaime." Mama whispered, and she could not say any more.

"And this, I know, is my own," said Papa of the next mat in the bundle. His mat was simple and the only colors on it were purple and gold.

"And this, for you, Marcelina."

I had always thought my name was too long. Now I was glad to see that my whole name was spelled out on the mat, even if the letters were small. Beneath my name was a lyre, done in three colors. Papa knew I loved music and played the piano. I was delighted with my new mat.

"And this is for you, José." José is my oldest brother. He wanted to become a doctor.

"This is yours, Antonio."

"And this, yours, Juan."

"And this is yours, Jesus."

One by one my brothers and sisters stepped forward to receive their mats. Mat after mat was unfolded. On each mat was a symbol that meant something special to each of us.

At last everyone was shown their mats. The air was filled with excited talk.

"You are not to use these mats until you go to the university," Papa said.

"But, Jaime," Mama said, wonderingly, "there are some more mats left in the bundle."

"Yes, there are *three* more mats to unfold. They are for the others who are not here...." Papa's voice grew soft and his eyes looked far away.

"I said I would bring home a sleeping mat for every one of the family. And so I did," Papa said. Then his eyes fell on each of us. "Do you think I'd forgotten them? Do you think I had forgotten them? Do you think I could forget them?

"This is for you, Josefina!

"And this, for you, Victoria!

"And this, for you, Concepcion!"

Papa's face was filled with a long-bewildered sorrow.

Then I understood. The mats were for my three sisters, who died when they were still very young.

After a long while, Papa broke the silence. "We must not ever forget them," he said softly. "They may be dead but they are never really gone. They are here, among us, always in our hearts."

The remaining mats were unfolded in silence. The colors were not bright but dull. I remember that the names of the dead among us did not glow or shine as did the other living names.

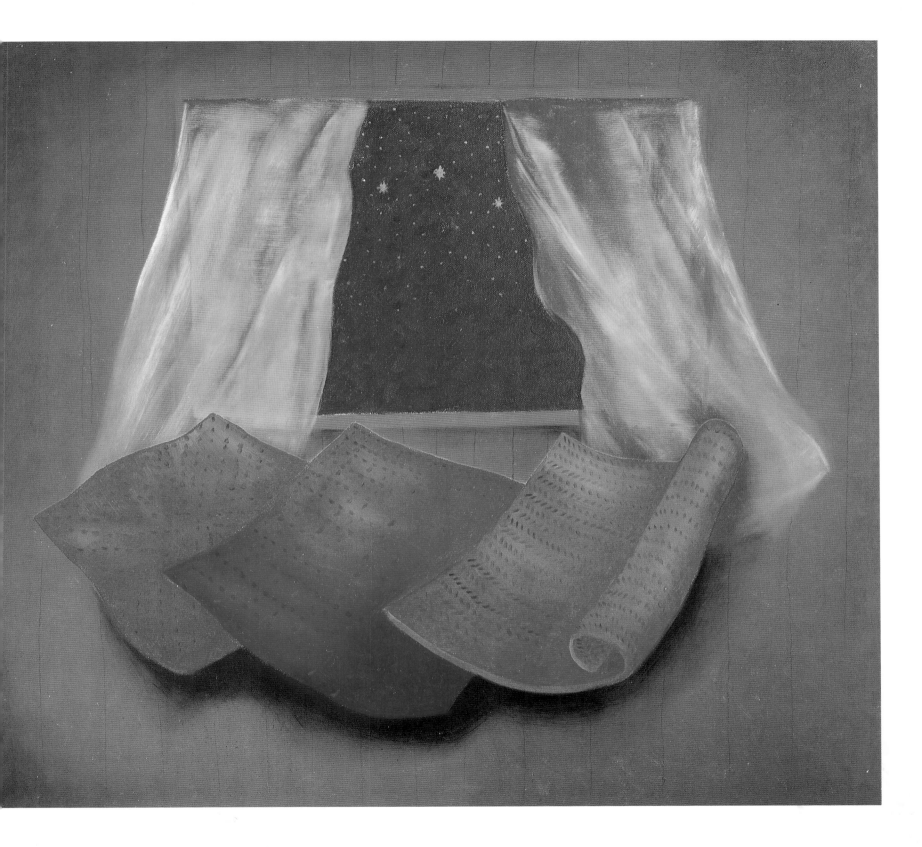

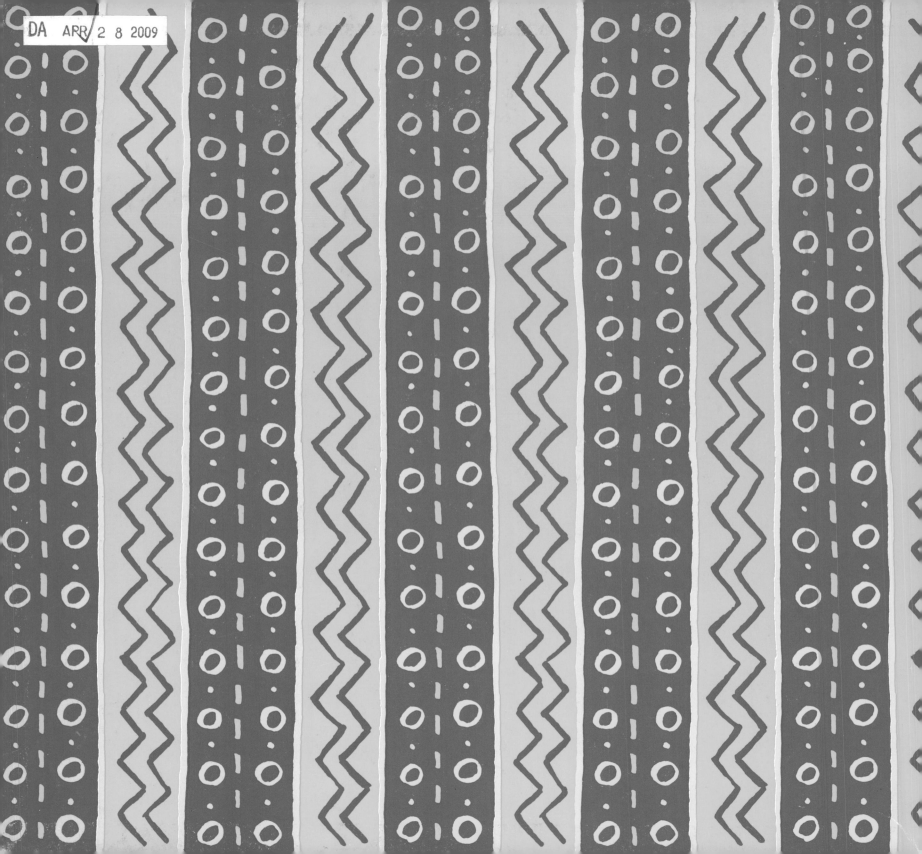